HORACE

by **HOLLY KELLER**

RED FOX

A Red Fox Book

Published by Random House Children's Books
20 Vauxhall Bridge Road, London SW1V 2SA

A division of Random House UK Ltd.
London Melbourne Sydney Auckland
Johannesburg and agencies throughout the world

First published in the USA by Greenwillow Books 1991
First published in Great Britain by Julia MacRae 1991

Red Fox edition 1993

© Holly Keller 1991

Printed in Hong Kong

ISBN 0 09 991110 8

FOR SUSAN

Horace lived in a small pink house with his parents.

He had his own room and his own toys. And every night at bedtime Mama told him the same story.

"We chose you when you were a tiny baby because you had lost your first family and needed a new one. We liked your spots, and we wanted you to be our child."

But Horace always fell asleep before Mama finished.

They were a fine family. Horace played draughts
with Papa every night, and Mama knitted him special
slippers so his feet would never be cold.

Sometimes when Mama made Horace eat his cereal and brush his teeth, or Papa made him wear his boots, Horace wished for different parents. But most of the time he was happy.

Mama planned a party for Horace's birthday.

"All your cousins are coming," she told him.

Mama made Horace's favourite stew. She baked a big birthday cake and everybody sang. But Horace was sad.

"My spots are silly," he said, looking around the table, "and I'm all the wrong colours."

Later he tried to turn his spots into stripes, but it didn't work.

Then he cut some pictures out of magazines
and hung them on the wall.

That night Mama tucked Horace into bed.

She patted his back and told him the same story as always.

"We chose you when you were a tiny baby because you had lost your first family and needed a new one. We liked your spots, and we wanted you to be our child."

And, as always, Horace fell asleep before the end.

He dreamed about being in a place
where everybody looked like him.

In the morning he stuffed some money and a few things into his pillowcase. He left a note on the fridge.

The park seemed a good place to begin.

A travelling fair had set up near the duck pond, and he bought some candy-floss. He was glad not to have anyone there to remind him that he would have to brush his teeth.

Then he got a ticket for the Ferris wheel.
"I'll be able to see everyone from the top," he told
the ticket man.
But when he looked down, everything was too small,
and his stomach felt awful.

The fair was crowded, so Horace took the boat across
the pond. He hummed a little song to help him feel brave.
Then he saw them. A big family, all spotted just like him,
was having a picnic under a tree.

Horace sat down on a bench and watched.

"Come and play with us," the littlest one called when

she noticed Horace sitting by himself.

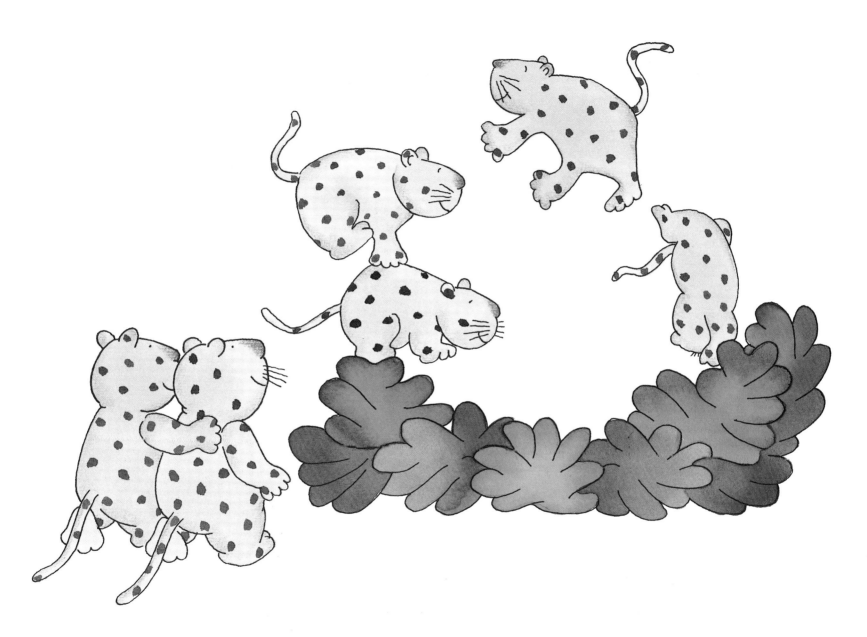

And Horace went to join the others.

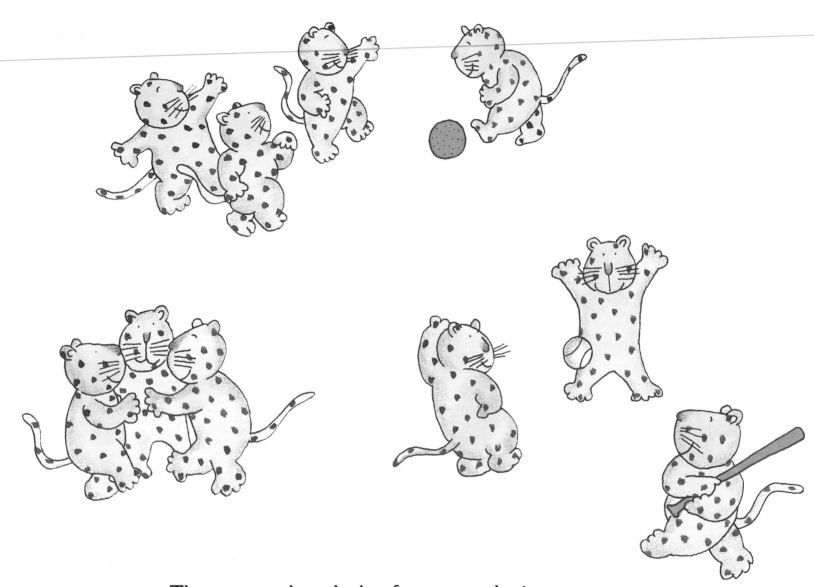

They spent the whole afternoon playing games.

Horace had fun, and he liked his new friends.

"Time for one more game before we go home," their mama called.

They played hide-and-seek. Horace hid behind a big rock.

He waited and waited.

The sun was going down and the air was chilly. Horace's feet felt cold. He thought about his slippers. He wondered if Papa was waiting for him to play draughts and if Mama missed him.

"Here he is!" somebody finally shouted, but
Horace didn't feel like playing any more.

"Come with us," his new friends said. Horace shook his head.

"I want to go home now," he said.

Horace caught the last boat back across the pond.

The fair was all shut down,
but Mama and Papa were there,
and they were looking for him.
In a flash he was in Mama's arms.

At bedtime Mama told Horace the story again. "We chose you

when you were a tiny baby because you had lost

your first family and needed a new one.

We liked your spots, and we wanted you to be our child."

And this time Horace listened all the way to the end.

"Mama," he said just before he closed his eyes,

"if you chose me, can I choose you, too?"

"That would be very nice," Mama said.

"Then I do," Horace whispered, and he was asleep.